To
the new big
brother, Andrew!
Enjoy the Spring!

From: Kristie
M°Cadden

The Twelve Days of Spring

WRITTEN AND ILLUSTRATED BY

Kristie McCadden

BARBOUR ROAD BOOKS
Hampton, New Hamphire

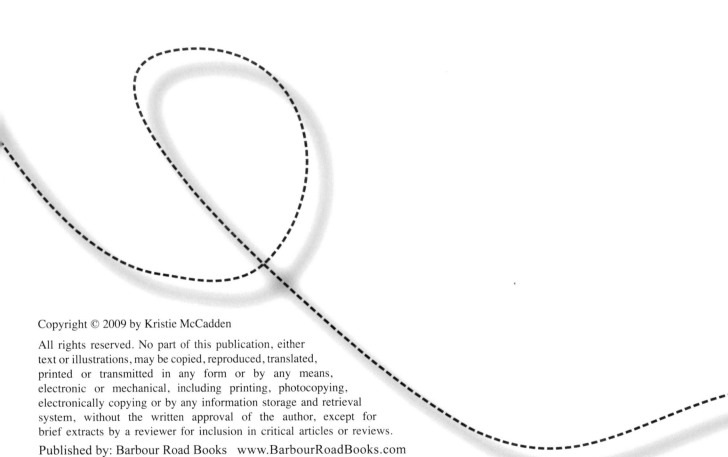

Published by: Barbour Road Books   www.BarbourRoadBooks.com

ISBN:978-096658271-0   Library of Congress PCN: 2008910343   10 9 8 7 6 5 4 3 2 1
Printed in China

For my husband, Troy, who believed in me and my dream,

for my children Cade and Maycie who gave me inspiration,

to all my family and friends who are such great support,

and to our little angel Mikey who is never far away!

I love you all!

INTRODUCTION

This wonderfully illustrated picture book will surely grab the attention of small children of all ages. It is based on the familiar song "The 12 days of Christmas". Little ones will love the repetitive sequence starting with one robin in an oak tree, two yawning bears, three daffodils…all the way up to twelve frogs-a-leaping. It is an accumulative counting rhyme about one of our four seasons – spring. You can use the questions and activities at the end of this book as a fun learning tool for your young audience.

ONE Robin in an oak tree.

1

On the third day of Spring
Mother Nature
gave to me...

THREE daffodils,
two yawning bears,
and a Robin in an
oak tree.

3

On the fourth day of Spring
Mother Nature gave to me...

FOUR hopping hares, three daffodils, two yawning bears, and a Robin in an oak tree.

4

On the fifth day of Spring
Mother Nature gave to me...

FIVE dragonflies,
four hopping hares,
three daffodils,
two yawning bears,
and a Robin in an oak tree.

5

On the sixth day of Spring
Mother Nature
gave to me...

SIX kites-a-flying,
five dragonflies,
four hopping hares,
three daffodils,
two yawning bears,
and a Robin in an oak tree.

6

On the seventh day of Spring
Mother Nature gave
to me...

SEVEN muddy puddles,
six kites-a-flying,
five dragonflies,
four hopping hares,
three daffodils,
two yawning bears,
and a Robin in an oak tree.

7

On the eighth day of Spring
Mother Nature gave to me...

8

EIGHT pussy willows,
seven muddy puddles,
six kites-a-flying,
five dragonflies,
four hopping hares,
three daffodils,
two yawning bears,
and a Robin in an oak tree.

On the ninth day of Spring
Mother Nature gave to me...

9

NINE bubbles blowing,
eight pussy willows,
seven muddy puddles,
six kites-a-flying,
five dragonflies,
four hopping hares,
three daffodils,
two yawning bears,
and a Robin in an oak tree.

On the tenth day of Spring
Mother Nature gave to me...

10

TEN bees-a-buzzing,
nine bubbles blowing,
eight pussy willows,
seven muddy puddles,
six kites-a-flying,
five dragonflies,
four hopping hares,
three daffodils, two yawning
bears, and a Robin in
an oak tree.

On the eleventh day of Spring
Mother Nature gave to me...

ELEVEN flags-a-waving
ten bees-a-buzzing,
nine bubbles blowing,
eight pussy willows,
seven muddy puddles,
six kites-a-flying,
five dragonflies,
four hopping hares,
three daffodils,
two yawning bears,
and a Robin in
an oak tree.

11

TWELVE frogs-a-leaping, eleven flags-a-waving, ten bees-a-buzzing, nine bubbles blowing, eight pussy willows, seven muddy puddles, six kites-a-flying, five dragonflies, four hopping hares, three daffodils, two yawning bears, and a Robin in an oak tree.

12

Questions and Activities

True or False: If a person touches a robin chick, the mother robin will abandon the chick.

False. Birds have a poor sense of smell. However, they have a great sense of sight and that is how they find their morning meal, the earth-worm.

What animals prey upon robins' chicks as well as their eggs?

Squirrels, Snakes and some birds such as Crows, Ravens and Blue Jays

Why are the two bears yawning?

Bears sleep in caves or dens all winter long because of the cold weather, and then wake up in spring when the weather is warmer. This is called hibernation.

Can you think of any other animals that hibernate?

Snakes, badgers, bees, chipmunks, frogs, turtles, woodchucks/ground-hogs, gophers, mice, raccoons, bats and skunks.

What is the difference between rabbits and hares?

Baby rabbits are born without any hair and with their eyes are closed. Baby hares are born with fur with their eyes opened. Rabbits make their home in underground burrows with lots of other rabbits and hares live above ground in nest-like homes with only a couple of other hares. Also, hares are a little larger than rabbits with longer ears.

Are dragonflies predators or prey?

Dragonflies are predators because they love to eat mosquitoes, flies, bees and even butterflies. They catch their prey in between their spike-studded legs.

If it's okay with mom…

Put on some old clothes and a pair of rain boots and go outside and jump in all the puddles you can find.

Find pussy willows.

If you have pussy willows near your home they are very pretty and look beautiful in a vase. Have an adult go with you to cut some for you and you can arrange them however you wish. If you have never touched a pussy willow, rub it softly on your face, they are extremely soft and it tickles too!

What are the bumble bees called that you see in early spring?

These are called the queen bees. They are the "mother" of all the bees in the hive. They are looking for nectar and pollen to turn into honey and food for their baby bees.

Go outside on a spring hunt.

See how many signs of the season you can find.

What animal comes out in the early spring and makes a loud "peep" noise?

Tree frogs that are called Spring Peepers. When there are a lot of them calling at the same time they can sound like sleigh bells.

Why do you only hear them at dusk or at night?

Because they are nocturnal (they sleep in the day and are awake at night). What is the opposite called, like you and me? We are awake in the day and we sleep at night; we are diurnal.

How many eggs can one Spring Peeper lay at once?

They can lay around 1,000 eggs. They lay them on twigs or at the bottom of ponds

The Twelve Days of Summer
The Twelve Days of Fall
The Twelve Days of Winter

For more information visit us at:

www.BarbourRoadBooks.com

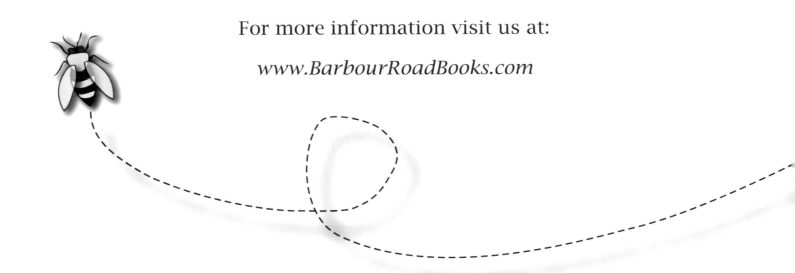